SHAKESPEARE RETOLD

Shakespeare Retold

By E. Nesbit

With a Foreword by John Lithgow

Illustrated by Antonio Javier Caparo

Biography and Timeline by Mariah Fredericks

HARPER

An Imprint of HarperCollinsPublishers

Shakespeare Retold

As told by E. Nesbit, adapted by Mariah Fredericks

Text copyright © 2016 by HarperCollins Publishers

Foreword copyright © 2016 by John Lithgow

Illustrations copyright © 2016 by Antonio Javier Caparo

All rights reserved. Manufactured in China.

No part of this book may be used or reproduced in any manner whatsoever without written permission except in the case of brief
quotations embodied in critical articles and reviews. For information address HarperCollins Children's Books, a division of
HarperCollins Publishers, 195 Broadway, New York, NY 10007.

www.harpercollinschildrens.com

ISBN 978-0-06-240453-4

The artist used Adobe Photoshop to create the digital illustrations for this book.

Typography by Jeanne Hogle

16 17 18 19 20   SCP   10 9 8 7 6 5 4 3 2 1

❖

First Edition

To Gabriela and Adriana—A.J.C.

CONTENTS

FOREWORD
by John Lithgow

I have a lucky history with Shakespeare, and I'll tell you why. When I was a boy, my father produced all of Shakespeare's plays at an outdoor summer festival in Yellow Springs, Ohio. He presented seven of them each season over the course of five years. Every summer my sister, my brother, and I would hang around the festival stage with our best friends. It was our version of summer camp. We befriended the grown-up actors and watched them rehearse. Sometimes we even played the kids' parts in the plays. My brother was one of Brutus's serving boys in *Julius Caesar*, my sister was a doomed prince in *Richard III*, and I was the fairy Mustardseed in *A Midsummer Night's Dream*.

Because of this early immersion, I knew a lot about Shakespeare long before he became a homework assignment for my tenth-grade English class. I knew him as a man of the theater, a great storyteller, an entertainer.

From the stage, I heard the crowds laugh and cry. At curtain calls, I heard their loud applause. As Mustardseed, I watched a company of actors experience the pure joy of playing Shakespeare's antic characters. I was just a child in the tiniest of roles, but I shared that joy with them.

Not surprisingly, my favorite scenes in those days were the most physical and theatrical. I loved the comic swordplay between Viola and Sir Andrew in *Twelfth Night* and the gory beheading at the end of *Macbeth.* No fewer than six times, I watched a memorable production of *Much Ado About Nothing.* Every time I eagerly awaited the entrance of Dogberry and his clownish night watchmen.

This was why I was so lucky. In my eyes, Shakespeare was glorious fun. His plays were the best stories of my childhood. I never completely understood the language of his dialogue (its wit, beauty, and power would finally hit me with blazing clarity in my mid-teens). But despite my young years, I had no trouble at all with Shakespeare's colorful characters and complex interlocking plots. His stories kept me on the edge of my seat for hours at a time, and I adored them.

Needless to say, not every child goes to Shakespeare summer camp. Few know the names of his most famous plays. Even fewer get a chance to see them performed, let alone perform in them. If they confront Shakespeare at all, it tends to happen in their high school years, by which time they have grown to dread him. This is why E. Nesbit's *Shakespeare Retold* is so welcome.

E. Nesbit has been called "the first modern writer for children." When they were published, books like *The Railway Children* and the many tales of the Bastable family were revolutionary in their utter lack of condescension toward the young. While occasionally dipping into the realm of the fantastical, she delighted in the adventures of real-life kids in real-life situations. In this regard, her literary descendants include C. S. Lewis, P. L. Travers, and J. K. Rowling. And although her books first appeared over a hundred years ago, her language is so clear and unadorned that they could have been written yesterday.

Who better than E. Nesbit to tell children the stories of Shakespeare's plays? There are seven of them here and her rendering of each flows like the engrossing storytelling of the Brothers Grimm. She doesn't neglect Shakespeare's language altogether. She deftly, almost teasingly throws in poetic phrases that make children want to hear even more. And just as seductive is the artwork of the book's illustrator, Antonio Javier Caparo. With a nod to Maxfield Parrish, his vivid images help children place these stories where they truly belong: in beautiful productions onstage, live in front of an audience.

As I said, I was lucky. I received an early education in Shakespeare without ever realizing I was being educated. By means of graceful prose and a knack for great storytelling, E. Nesbit has offered the same gift to young people.

John Lithgow

ROMEO AND JULIET

ROMEO AND JULIET

O Romeo, Romeo, wherefore art thou Romeo?

CAST OF CHARACTERS

LORD AND LADY MONTAGUE
heads of the house of Montague

ROMEO MONTAGUE

MERCUTIO AND BENVOLIO
Romeo's friends

LORD AND LADY CAPULET
heads of the house of Capulet

JULIET CAPULET

NURSE
the woman who looks after Juliet

TYBALT
Juliet's cousin

COUNT PARIS
the prince's relative and Juliet's suitor

FRIAR LAURENCE

SCENE

VERONA, ITALY

nce upon a time there lived in Verona two great families named Montague and Capulet. They were both rich, and I suppose they were as sensible, in most things, as other rich people. But in one thing they were extremely silly. There was an old, old quarrel between the two families, and instead of making up, they made a sort of pet of their quarrel and would not let it die. A Montague wouldn't speak to a Capulet if they met in the street, nor a Capulet to a Montague. If they did speak, it was to say rude and unpleasant things, which often ended in a fight. Their relatives and servants were just as foolish, so that street fights and duels were always growing out of the Montague-and-Capulet quarrel.

Now, Lord Capulet, the head of that family, gave a party, a grand supper and dance. He said anyone might come to it except (of course) the Montagues. But there was a young Montague named Romeo who very much wanted to go, because Rosaline, the lady he loved, would be there. This lady had never been at all kind to him, and he had no reason to love her. But the fact was that he wanted to love somebody, and as he hadn't seen the right lady, he was obliged to love the wrong one. So to the Capulets' grand party he went, with his friends Mercutio and Benvolio. (All three wore masks so they would not be discovered as the hated Montagues.)

Old Capulet welcomed Romeo and his two friends very kindly. Young Romeo moved about among the crowd of courtly folk dressed in their velvets and satins. The men wore jeweled sword hilts and collars. The ladies had brilliant gems on their breasts and arms, and more gemstones set in their bright dresses. Romeo was in his best too, and though he wore a black mask, everyone could see by his mouth and his hair, and by the way he held his head, that he was twelve times handsomer than anyone else in the room.

Then among the dancers he saw a lady so beautiful and so lovable that from that moment on, he never gave another thought to Rosaline. As he looked at this fair lady, dancing in her white satin and pearls, all the world seemed vain and worthless compared with her.

He said this, or something like it, and Tybalt, Lady Capulet's nephew, hearing his voice, knew him to be Romeo. In a rage, Tybalt went at once to his uncle and told him that a Montague had come uninvited to the feast. Old Capulet was too fine a gentleman to be rude to any man under his own roof, and he told Tybalt to be quiet. But this young man watched for his chance to quarrel with Romeo.

In the meantime, Romeo made his way to the fair lady. He told her in sweet words that he loved her and kissed her. Just then her mother sent for her. It was then that Romeo found out that the lady on whom he had set his heart's hopes was Juliet, the daughter of Lord Capulet, his sworn foe. So he went away, sorrowing but loving her nonetheless.

Juliet said to her nurse: "Who is that gentleman that would not dance?"

"His name is Romeo, and a Montague, the only son of your great enemy," answered the nurse.

Then Juliet went to her room and looked out her window over the beautiful green-gray garden, where the moon was shining. Romeo was hidden in that garden among the trees—because he could not bear to go away without trying to see her again. Juliet—not knowing he was there—spoke her secret thought aloud and told the quiet garden how she loved Romeo.

And Romeo heard her and was glad beyond measure. Hidden below, he saw her fair face in the moonlight, framed in the blossoming creepers that grew around her window. And as he looked and listened, he felt as though he had been carried away in a dream and set down by some magician in that beautiful and enchanted garden.

"Ah—why are you called Romeo?" said Juliet. "Since I love you, what does it matter what you are called?"

"Call me but love, and I'll be new baptized. Henceforth I never will be Romeo," he cried, stepping into the full white moonlight from the shadows of the cypresses and oleanders that had hidden him.

Juliet was frightened at first, but when she saw that it was Romeo, and no stranger, she too was glad. He standing in the garden below and she leaning from the window, they spoke long together, each one trying to find the sweetest words in the world, to make that pleasant talk that lovers use. (The tale of all they said, and the sweet music their voices made, is all set down in a golden book, where you children may read it for yourselves someday.)

And the time passed so quickly, as it does for folk who love each other and are together, that when the time came to part, it seemed as though they had met but that moment. Indeed, they hardly knew how to part.

"Send word to me tomorrow," said Juliet.

At last, with lingering and longing, they said good-bye.

Juliet went into her room, and a dark curtain hid her bright window.

Romeo went away through the still and dewy garden like a man in a dream.

The next morning, very early, Romeo went to Friar Laurence, a priest, and told him the whole story. He begged the friar to marry him and Juliet without delay. And this, after some talk, the priest consented to do.

So when Juliet sent her old nurse to Romeo that day to know what he intended, the old woman took back a message that all things were ready for the marriage of Juliet and Romeo on the next morning.

The young lovers were afraid to ask for their parents' consent to their marriage because of this foolish old quarrel between the Capulets and the Montagues. Friar Laurence was willing to help the young lovers because he thought that when they were married, the match might put a happy end to the old quarrel.

So the next morning early, Romeo and Juliet were married in Friar Laurence's cell. They parted with tears and kisses. Romeo promised to come to the garden that evening. The nurse got ready a rope ladder to let down from the window so that Romeo could climb up and talk to his dear wife.

But that very day a dreadful thing happened.

Tybalt, the young man who was so vexed at Romeo's coming to the Capulets' feast, met Romeo and his two friends Mercutio and Benvolio in the street. Tybalt called Romeo a villain and asked him to fight. Romeo had no wish to fight with Juliet's cousin, but Mercutio drew his sword, and he and Tybalt fought. Mercutio was killed. When Romeo saw that his friend was dead, he forgot everything except anger at the man who had killed him. He and Tybalt fought till Tybalt fell dead.

So on the very day of his wedding, Romeo killed his dear Juliet's cousin and was sentenced to be banished. Poor Juliet and her young husband met that night, but their meeting was a sad one, and they parted with bitter tears and hearts heavy, not knowing when they would meet again.

Now, Juliet's father, who of course had no idea that she was married, wished her to wed a gentleman named Paris. He was so angry when she refused that Juliet hurried away to ask Friar Laurence what she should do. He advised her to pretend to consent. And then he said:

"I will give you a potion that will make you seem to be dead for two days, and then when they take you to church, it will be to bury you and not to marry you. They will put you in the tomb, thinking you are dead, and before you wake up, Romeo and I will be there to take care of you. Will you do this, or are you afraid?"

"I will do it; talk not to me of fear!" said Juliet. And she went home and told her father she would marry Paris. If she had only told her father the truth . . . well, then this would have been a different story.

Lord Capulet was very much pleased and set about inviting his friends and getting the wedding feast ready. Everyone stayed up all night, for there was a great deal to do and very little time in which to do it. Lord Capulet was anxious to get Juliet married because he saw she was very unhappy. Of course she was really fretting about her husband, Romeo; but her father thought she was grieving for the death of her cousin Tybalt, and he thought marriage would give her something else to think about.

Early in the morning the nurse came to dress Juliet for her wedding, but she would not wake. At last the nurse cried out—

"Alas! Alas! Help! Help! My lady's dead! Oh, well-a-day, that ever I was born!"

Lady Capulet came running in, and then Lord Capulet, and Lord Paris, the bridegroom. There lay Juliet, cold and white and lifeless. All their weeping could not wake her. So it was a burying that day instead of a marrying.

Meantime Friar Laurence had sent a messenger with a letter to Romeo

telling him of the plan. All would have been well—but the messenger was delayed and could not go.

Ill news travels fast. Romeo's servant, who knew of Romeo and Juliet's marriage, heard of her funeral and hurried to tell Romeo how his young wife was dead and lying in the grave.

"Is it so?" cried Romeo, heartbroken. "Then I will lie by Juliet's side tonight."

He bought himself a poison and went straight back to Verona. He hastened to the tomb where Juliet was lying. He broke open the door and was just going down the stone steps that led to the vault where all the dead Capulets lay when he heard a voice calling for him to stop.

It was Count Paris, who was to have married Juliet that very day.

"How dare you come here and disturb the dead bodies of the Capulets, you vile Montague?" cried Paris.

Poor Romeo was half mad with sorrow, yet he tried to answer gently.

"You were told," said Paris, "that if you returned to Verona you must die."

"I must indeed," said Romeo. "I came here for nothing else. Good, gentle youth—leave me! Oh, go—before I do you any harm! I love you better than myself—go—leave me here—"

Then Paris said, "I defy you, and I arrest you as a criminal."

Romeo, in his anger and despair, drew his sword. They fought, and Paris was killed.

As Romeo's sword pierced him, Paris cried, "Oh, I am slain! If thou be merciful, open the tomb, and lay me with Juliet!"

And Romeo said, "In faith, I will."

And he carried the dead man into the tomb and laid him by dear Juliet's side. Then he knelt by Juliet and spoke to her. He held her in his arms and kissed her cold lips, believing that she was dead—but all the while she was coming nearer and nearer to the time of her awakening. Then he drank the poison and died beside his sweetheart and wife.

Now came Friar Laurence when it was too late. Poor Juliet woke from her sleep to find her husband and her friend both dead beside her.

The noise of the fight had brought other folks to the tomb. Hearing them, Friar Laurence ran away, and Juliet was left alone. She saw the vial that had held the poison and knew how all had happened. Since no poison was left for her, she drew Romeo's dagger and thrust it through her heart—and so, falling with her head on her Romeo's breast, she died.

And here ends the story of these faithful and most unhappy lovers.

When the Capulets and Montagues learned from Friar Laurence all that had happened, they were deeply sad. Seeing the mischief their wicked quarrel had caused, they repented, and over the bodies of their dead children they clasped hands at last, in friendship and forgiveness.

A MIDSUMMER
NIGHT'S DREAM

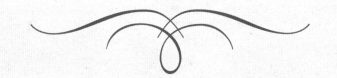

A MIDSUMMER NIGHT'S DREAM

The course of true love never did run smooth.

CAST OF CHARACTERS

Hermia
a young noblewoman who loves Lysander

Lysander
Hermia's beloved

Demetrius
a young noble also in love with Hermia

Helena
Hermia's friend who loves Demetrius

Oberon
king of the fairies

Titania
queen of the fairies

Puck
Oberon's favorite fairy servant—a mischevious sprite

Bottom
a weaver

Peaseblossom, Cobweb, Moth, and Mustardseed
fairy attendants

SCENE

Ancient Athens, Greece

ermia and Lysander were lovers. But Hermia's father wished her to marry another man named Demetrius.

Now, in Athens, where they lived, there was a wicked law by which any girl who refused to marry according to her father's wishes might be put to death. Hermia's father was so angry with her for refusing to do as he wished that he actually brought her before the duke of Athens to ask that she might be killed. The duke gave her four days to think about it. At the end of that time, if she still refused to marry Demetrius, she would die.

Lysander of course was nearly mad with grief. He decided the best thing to do was for Hermia to run away to his aunt's house, which lay beyond the reach of that cruel law. There he would come to her and marry her. But before she started, Hermia told her friend Helena what she was going to do.

Helena had been Demetrius's sweetheart long before he'd fallen in love with Hermia. Being very silly, like all jealous people, she could not see that it was not poor Hermia's fault that Demetrius wished to marry her instead of Helena. She knew that if she told Demetrius that Hermia was going to the wood outside Athens, he would follow her. "And I can follow him, and at least I shall see him," she said to herself. So she went to Demetrius and betrayed her friend's secret.

This wood where Lysander was to meet Hermia, and where the other two had decided to follow them, was full of fairies, as most woods are, if one only has the eyes to see them. And in this wood on this night were the king and queen of the fairies, Oberon and Titania. Fairies are very wise people, but now and then they can be quite as foolish as mortal folk. Oberon and Titania, who could have been as happy as the days were long, had thrown away all their joy in a foolish quarrel. They never met without saying disagreeable things to each other, scolding each other so dreadfully that all their little fairy followers would creep into acorn cups and hide there out of fear.

So instead of having one happy court and dancing all night through in the moonlight as is fairies' custom, the king with his attendants wandered through one part of the wood while the queen with hers lived in another. The cause of all this trouble was a little Indian boy whom Titania had taken to be one of her followers. Oberon wanted the child to be one of his fairy knights, but the queen would not give him up.

On this night, in a mossy moonlit glade, the king and queen of the fairies met.

"Ill met by moonlight, proud Titania," said the king.

"What, jealous Oberon?" answered the queen. "You spoil everything with your quarreling. Come, fairies, let us leave him. I am not friends with him now."

"It rests with you to make up the quarrel," said the king. "Give me that little Indian boy, and I will again be your humble servant and suitor."

"Set your heart at rest," said the queen. "Your whole fairy kingdom buys not that boy from me. Come, fairies."

And she and her train rode off down the moonbeams.

"Well, go your way," said Oberon. "But I'll be even with you before you leave this wood."

Then Oberon called his favorite fairy, Puck. Puck was the spirit of mischief. He used to slip into dairies and take the cream away. He would get into the churn so that the butter would not come, turn the beer sour, and lead people out of their way on dark nights and laugh at them. He would tumble people's stools from under them when they were going to sit down, and upset their hot ale over their chins when they were going to drink.

"Now," said Oberon to this little sprite, "fetch me the flower called Love-in-idleness. The juice of that little purple flower laid on the eyes of those who sleep will make them, when they wake, to love the first thing they see. I will put some of the juice of that flower on my Titania's eyes, and when she wakes, she will love the first thing she sees, be it lion, bear, or wolf, or bull, or meddling monkey, or a busy ape."

While Puck was gone, Demetrius passed through the glade followed by poor Helena. Over and over she told him how she loved him and reminded him of his promises to her. Still he told her that he did not and could not love her, and that his promises were nothing. Oberon was sorry for poor Helena, and when Puck returned with the flower, he bade him follow Demetrius and put some of the juice on his eyes so that he might love Helena when he woke and looked on her. So Puck set off.

Wandering through the wood, he found not Demetrius but Lysander, on whose eyes he put the juice. But when Lysander woke, he saw not his

own Hermia but Helena, who was walking through the wood looking for the cruel Demetrius. And the moment he saw her he loved her and left his own lady, under the spell of the purple flower.

When Hermia woke she found Lysander gone, and she wandered about the wood trying to find him. Puck went back and told Oberon what he had done. Oberon soon saw that Puck had made a mistake, so he set about looking for Demetrius. Having found him, he put some of the juice on his eyes. The first thing Demetrius saw when he woke was also Helena. So now Demetrius and Lysander were both following her through the wood, and it was Hermia's turn to follow her lover as Helena had done before. The end of it was that Helena and Hermia began to quarrel, and Demetrius and Lysander went off to fight. Oberon was very sorry to see his kind scheme to help these lovers turn out so badly. So he said to Puck:

"These two young men are going to fight. You must fill the night with drooping fog and lead them so astray that one will never find the other. When they are tired out, they will fall asleep. Then drop this other herb on Lysander's eyes. That will give him his old sight and his old love. Then each man will have the lady who loves him, and they will all think that this has been only a midsummer night's dream. Then when this is done, all will be well with them."

So Puck went and did as he was told, and when the two had fallen asleep without meeting each other, Puck poured the juice on Lysander's eyes and said:

When thou wakest,
Thou takest
True delight
In the sight
Of thy former lady's eye: . . .
Jack shall have Jill;
Nought shall go ill.

Meanwhile Oberon found Titania asleep on a bank where grew wild thyme, oxlips, and violets, and woodbine, musk-roses, and eglantine. Titania always slept a part of the night there, wrapped in the enameled skin of a snake. Oberon stooped over her and laid the juice on her eyes, saying:

What thou seest when thou wake,
Do it for thy true love take.

Now, when Titania woke, the first thing she saw was a villager, one of a party of players who had come into the wood to rehearse their play. This foolish man was named Bottom, and he had already met with Puck, who had placed an ass's head on his shoulders so that it looked as if it grew there. When Titania woke and saw this dreadful monster, she said, "What angel is this? Are you as wise as you are beautiful?"

"If I am wise enough to find my way out of this wood, that's enough for me," said the villager.

"Do not desire to go out of the wood," said Titania. The spell of the love-juice was on her, and to her the furry-eared Bottom seemed the most beautiful and delightful creature on all the earth. "I love you," she went on. "Come with me, and I will give you fairies to attend on you."

So she called four fairies, whose names were Peaseblossom, Cobweb, Moth, and Mustardseed.

"You must attend this gentleman," said the queen. "Feed him with apricots and dewberries, purple grapes, green figs, and mulberries. Steal honey-bags for him from the bumblebees, and with the wings of painted butterflies fan the moon-beams from his sleeping eyes."

"I will," said one of the fairies, and all the others said, "I will."

"Now, sit down with me," said the queen, "and let me stroke your dear cheeks, and stick musk-roses in your sleek smooth head, and kiss your fair large ears, my gentle joy."

"Where's Peaseblossom?" asked Bottom. He did not care much about the queen's affection, but he was very proud of having fairies to wait on him.

"Ready," said Peaseblossom.

"Scratch my head, Peaseblossom," said Bottom. "Where's Cobweb?"

"Ready," said Cobweb.

"Kill," said Bottom, "the red bumblebee on the top of the thistle yonder, and bring me the honey-bag. Where's Mustardseed?"

"Ready," said Mustardseed.

"Oh, I want nothing," said Bottom. "Only just help Cobweb to scratch. I must go to the barber's, for methinks I am marvelous hairy about the face."

"Would you like anything to eat?" said the fairy queen.

"I should like some good dry oats," said Bottom, for his donkey's head made him desire donkey's food, "and some hay to follow."

"Shall some of my fairies fetch you new nuts from the squirrel's house?" asked the queen.

"I'd rather have a handful or two of good dried peas," said Bottom. "But please don't let any of your people disturb me; I am going to sleep."

Then said the queen, "And I will wind thee in my arms."

And so when Oberon came along, he found his beautiful queen lavishing kisses and endearments on an idiot with a donkey's head.

Before he released her from the enchantment, he persuaded her to give him the little Indian boy he so desired to have. Then he took pity on her and threw some juice of the disenchanting flower on her pretty eyes. In a moment she saw plainly the donkey-headed villager she had loved and knew how foolish she had been.

Oberon took off the ass's head from the man and left him to finish his sleep with his own silly head lying on the thyme and violets.

Thus all was made plain and straight again. Oberon and Titania loved each other more than ever. Demetrius thought of no one but Helena, and Helena had never had any thought of anyone but Demetrius.

As for Hermia and Lysander, they were as loving a couple as you could meet in a day's walk, even through a fairy wood.

So the four mortal lovers went back to Athens and were married. And the fairy king and queen live happily together in that very wood to this very day.

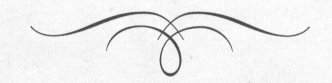

TWELFTH NIGHT

TWELFTH NIGHT

If music be the food of love, play on.

CAST OF CHARACTERS

VIOLA
a young noblewoman disguised as a gentleman called Cesario

SEBASTIAN
Viola's identical twin brother

ORSINO
duke of Illyria

OLIVIA
a countess

MARIA
Olivia's servant

MALVOLIO
Olivia's steward

SIR TOBY BELCH
Olivia's uncle

SIR ANDREW AGUECHEEK
Olivia's suitor

SCENE

ILLYRIA, ON THE EASTERN COAST OF THE ADRIATIC SEA

rsino, the duke of Illyria, was deeply in love with a beautiful countess named Olivia. Yet his love was in vain, for she did not care for him. When her brother died, she sent back a messenger from the duke, commanding him to tell his master that for seven years she would not let even the air behold her face. Like a nun, she would walk veiled—all for the sake of a dead brother's love, which she would keep fresh and lasting in her sad remembrance.

The duke longed for someone to whom he could tell his sorrow. Chance brought him such a companion. For about this time a goodly ship was wrecked on the Illyrian coast, and among those who reached land in safety were the captain and a fair young maid named Viola. But she was not grateful for being rescued from the perils of the sea since she feared that her twin brother, Sebastian, was drowned. He was as dear to

her as the heart in her bosom and so like her that, but for the difference in their manner of dress, one could hardly be told from the other. The captain, for her comfort, told her that he had seen her brother bind himself "to a strong mast that lived upon the sea," and that there was hope that he might have been saved.

Viola now asked in whose country she was. Learning that the young Duke Orsino, who was as noble in his nature as in his name, ruled there, she decided to disguise herself in male attire and seek employment with him as a page.

In this she succeeded, and from day to day she had to listen to the story of Orsino's love. At first she sympathized with him, but soon her sympathy grew into love. It occurred to Orsino that his hopeless love suit might prosper better if he sent this pretty lad to woo Olivia for him. Viola unwillingly went on this errand. But when she came to the house, Malvolio, Olivia's steward, a vain, officious man, forbade Viola admittance.

But Viola (who was now called Cesario), refused to take any denial and vowed to speak with the countess. Olivia, hearing how her instructions were defied and curious to see this daring youth, said, "We'll once more hear Orsino's plea."

When Viola was admitted to her presence and the servants had been sent away, Olivia listened patiently to the words of love that this bold messenger from the duke poured upon her. Listening, she fell in love with the supposed Cesario. When Cesario had gone, Olivia longed to send him a love token. So, calling Malvolio, she bade him follow the boy.

"He left this ring," she said, taking one from her finger. "Tell him I will have none of it."

Malvolio did as he was told. Viola, who of course knew perfectly well that she had left no ring behind, saw with a woman's quickness that Olivia loved her. Then she went back to the duke, very sad at heart for him, and for Olivia, and for herself.

It was but cold comfort she could give Orsino, who now sought to ease the pangs of despised love by listening to sweet music while Cesario stood by his side.

"Ah," said the duke to his page that night, "you too have been in love."

"A little," answered Viola.

"What kind of woman is it?" he asked.

"Of your complexion," she answered.

"What years, i' faith?" was his next question.

To this came the pretty answer, "About your years, my lord."

"Too old, by heaven!" cried the duke. "Let still the woman take someone older than herself."

And Viola very meekly said, "I think it well, my lord."

By and by Orsino begged Cesario once more to visit Olivia and to plead his love suit. But she, thinking to change his mind, said, "If some lady loved you as you love Olivia?"

"Ah! That cannot be," said the duke.

"But I know," Viola went on, "what love woman may have for a man. My father had a daughter loved a man, as it might be." She added, blushing, "Perhaps, were I a woman, I should love your lordship."

"And what is her history?" he asked.

"A blank, my lord," Viola answered. "She never told her love, but let concealment, like a worm in the bud, feed on her damask cheek: she pined in thought, and with a green and yellow melancholy she sat, like Patience on a monument, smiling at grief. Was not this love indeed?"

"But died thy sister of her love, my boy?" the duke asked; and Viola, who had all this time been telling her own love for him in this pretty fashion, said:

"I am all the daughters my father has and all the brothers. Sir, shall I go to the lady?"

"To her in haste," said the duke, at once forgetting all about the story, "and give her this jewel."

So Viola went, still dressed as a man, and this time poor Olivia was unable to hide her love. She openly confessed it with such passionate truth that Viola left her hastily, saying, "Nevermore will I report my master's tears to you."

But Viola did not know the tender pity she would feel for another's suffering. So when Olivia sent a messenger, praying Cesario to visit her once more, Cesario had no heart to refuse the request.

The favors that Olivia bestowed on this mere page aroused the jealousy of Sir Andrew Aguecheek, a foolish rejected lover of hers. At that time he was staying at her house with her merry old uncle Sir Toby. This same Sir Toby dearly loved a practical joke, and knowing Sir Andrew to be a complete coward, he thought that if he could arrange a duel between him and Cesario, there would be rare sport indeed. So he persuaded Sir Andrew to send a challenge, which he himself took to Cesario. The poor page, in great terror, said, "I will return again to the house. I am no fighter."

"Back you shall not to the house," said Sir Toby, "unless you fight me first."

As Sir Toby looked a very fierce old gentleman, Viola thought it best to await Sir Andrew. When he at last made his appearance—in a great fright, if the truth be known—Viola tremblingly drew her sword, and a terrified Sir Andrew followed her example. Happily for them both, some officers of the court came on the scene and stopped the intended duel. Viola gladly ran off, while Sir Toby called after her, "A very paltry boy, and more a coward than a hare!"

Now, while these things were happening, Viola's brother, Sebastian, had escaped the dangers of the deep and had landed safely in Illyria. He too decided to make his way to the duke's court. On his way there he passed Olivia's house, and whom should he meet but Sir Andrew and Sir Toby. Sir Andrew, mistaking Sebastian for the cowardly Cesario, struck him, saying, "There's for you."

"Why, there's for you; and there, and there!" said Sebastian, hitting back a great deal harder. He hit Sir Andrew again and again, till Sir Toby came to the rescue of his friend. Sebastian, however, tore himself free from Sir Toby's clutches and, drawing his sword, would have fought them both. But Olivia, hearing the quarrel, came running out and, with many reproaches, sent Sir Toby and his friend away. Then, turning to Sebastian, whom she thought to be Cesario, she begged him with many a pretty speech to come into the house with her.

Sebastian, half dazed and all delighted with her beauty and grace, readily consented. That very day, so great was Olivia's haste, they were married before she had discovered that he was not Cesario.

Meanwhile Orsino, hearing how ill Cesario had fared with Olivia, visited her himself, taking Cesario with him. Olivia met them both at her door and, seeing the man she thought to be her husband, reproached him for leaving her. To the duke she said that his pleas sounded as unpleasant to her as the sound of howling after music.

"Still so cruel?" said Orsino.

"Still so constant," she answered.

Then Orsino's anger turned cruel. He vowed that in revenge he would kill Cesario, whom he knew she loved. "Come, boy," he said to the page.

Following him, Viola said, "I, for your pleasure, a thousand deaths would die."

A great fear took hold of Olivia, and she cried aloud, "Cesario, husband, stay!"

"Her husband?" asked the duke angrily.

"No, my lord, not I," said Viola.

"Call forth the holy father," cried Olivia.

And the priest who had married Sebastian and Olivia came and declared Cesario to be the bridegroom.

"O thou dissembling cub!" the duke exclaimed. "Farewell, and take her; but go where thou and I henceforth may never meet."

At this moment a bleeding Sir Andrew came up and complained that Cesario had broken his head, and Sir Toby's as well.

"I never hurt you," said Viola very positively; "you drew your sword on me, but I hurt you not."

Yet, for all her protesting, no one there believed her. But all their thoughts were changed to wonder when Sebastian came in.

"I am sorry, madam," he said to his wife. "I have hurt your kinsman. Pardon me, sweet one, especially given the vows we made each other so recently."

"One face, one voice, one habit, and two persons!" cried the duke, looking first at Viola and then at Sebastian.

"An apple cleft in two," said one who knew Sebastian, "is not more twin than these two creatures. Which is Sebastian?"

"I never had a brother," said Sebastian. "I had a sister, whom the blind waves and surges have devoured. Were you a woman," he said to Viola, "I should let my tears fall upon your cheek, and say 'Thrice-welcome, drowned Viola!'"

Then Viola, rejoicing to see her dear brother alive, confessed that she was indeed his sister. As she spoke, Orsino felt the pity that is close to love.

"Boy," he said, "thou hast said to me a thousand times thou never shouldst love woman as much as me."

"And all those sayings will I overswear," Viola replied, "and those swearings keep true."

"Give me thy hand," Orsino cried in gladness. "Thou shalt be my wife, and my fancy's queen."

Thus was gentle Viola made happy, while Olivia found in Sebastian a constant lover and a good husband, and he in her a true and loving wife.

HAMLET

HAMLET

To be or not to be: that is the question.

✧

This above all: to thine own self be true.

CAST OF CHARACTERS

HAMLET
prince of Denmark

KING CLAUDIUS
Hamlet's uncle

QUEEN GERTRUDE
Hamlet's mother

HORATIO
Hamlet's friend

POLONIUS
counselor to the king

OPHELIA
daughter of Polonius

LAERTES
son of Polonius

SCENE

DENMARK

amlet was the only son of the king of Denmark. He loved his father and mother dearly—and was happy in the love of a sweet lady named Ophelia. Her father, Polonius, was the king's chamberlain.

While Hamlet was away studying at Wittenberg, his father died. Young Hamlet hastened home in great grief to hear that a serpent had stung the king and killed him. The young prince had loved his father so tenderly that you can guess what he felt when he found that the queen, before the king had been in the ground a month, had decided to marry again—and to marry the dead king's brother.

Hamlet refused to take off his black mourning clothes for the wedding.

"It is not only the black I wear on my body," he said, "that proves my loss. I wear mourning in my heart for my dead father. His son at least remembers him, and grieves still."

Then said Claudius, the king's brother, "This grief is unreasonable. Of course you must sorrow at the loss of your father, but—"

"Ah," said Hamlet bitterly, "I cannot in one little month forget those I love."

With that the queen and Claudius left him to make merry over their wedding, forgetting the poor good dead king who had been so kind to them both.

Hamlet, left alone, wondered what he ought to do. For he could not believe the story about the snakebite. It seemed to him all too plain that the wicked Claudius had killed the king so as to get the crown and marry the queen. Yet he had no proof and could not accuse Claudius.

While he was thinking, Horatio, a fellow student, arrived from Wittenberg.

"What brought you here?" asked Hamlet when he had greeted his friend kindly.

"I came, my lord, to see your father's funeral."

"I think it was to see my mother's wedding," said Hamlet bitterly. "My father! We shall not look upon his like again."

"My lord," answered Horatio, "I think I saw him yesternight."

Then Horatio told how he, with two gentlemen of the guard, had seen the king's ghost on the castle battlements. Hamlet went that night, and true enough, at midnight, the ghost of the king appeared in the chill moonlight. Hamlet was a brave youth. Instead of running away from the ghost, Hamlet spoke to it— and when it beckoned him, he followed it to a quiet place. There the ghost told him that what Hamlet had suspected was true. The wicked Claudius had indeed killed his good brother the king by dropping poison into his ear as he slept in his orchard in the afternoon.

"And you," said the ghost, "must avenge this cruel murder by my wicked brother. But do nothing against the queen—for I have loved her, and she is your mother. Remember me."

Then, seeing the morning approach, the ghost vanished.

"Now," said Hamlet, "there is nothing left but revenge. Remember thee—I will remember nothing else—books, pleasure, youth—let all go—and your commands alone live in my brain."

When his friend came back, he made him swear to keep the secret of the ghost. Then he went in from the battlements, now gray with mingled dawn and moonlight, to think how he might best avenge his murdered father.

The shock of seeing his father's ghost made him feel almost mad. For fear that his uncle might notice that he was not himself, he decided to hide his longing for revenge under a pretended madness.

So when he met Ophelia, who loved him—and to whom he had given gifts, and letters, and many loving words—he behaved so wildly to her that she could not but think him mad. For she loved him and she could not believe he would be as cruel as this, unless he were quite mad. So she told her father and showed him a letter from Hamlet. And in the letter was this pretty verse—

Doubt thou the stars are fire,
Doubt that the sun doth move,
Doubt truth to be a liar,
But never doubt I love.

And from that time everyone believed that the cause of Hamlet's supposed madness was love.

Poor Hamlet was very unhappy. He longed to obey his father's ghost—and yet he was too gentle and kindly to wish to kill another man, even his father's murderer. Sometimes he wondered whether, after all, the ghost had told the truth.

Just at this time some actors came to the court. Hamlet ordered them to perform a certain play before the king and queen. Now, this play was the story of a man who had been murdered in his garden by a relative who afterward married the dead man's wife.

You may imagine the feelings of the wicked king as he sat on his throne, with the queen beside him and all his court, and saw, acted on the stage, the very wickedness that he had himself done. When, in the play, the wicked relative poured poison into the ear of the sleeping man, the wicked Claudius suddenly rose and staggered from the room—the queen and others following.

Hamlet said to his friends, "I am sure the ghost spoke true. For if Claudius had not done this murder, he would not have been so distressed to see it in a play."

Now the queen sent for Hamlet to scold him for his behavior. Claudius, wishing to know exactly what happened, told old Polonius to hide himself behind the hangings in the queen's room. As they talked, the queen got frightened at Hamlet's rough, strange words and cried for help. Polonius, behind the curtain, cried out too. Hamlet, thinking it was Claudius who was hidden there, thrust with his sword at the hangings and killed not the king but poor old Polonius.

"Oh! What a rash and bloody deed is this," cried the queen.

And Hamlet answered bitterly, "Almost as bad as to kill a king and marry his brother." Then Hamlet told the queen plainly all his thoughts and how he knew of the murder. He begged her to have no more friendship with the base Claudius, who had killed the good king. As they spoke, the king's ghost again appeared before Hamlet, but the queen could not see it. When the ghost had gone, Hamlet and the queen parted.

When the queen told Claudius what had passed and how Polonius was dead, he said, "This shows plainly that Hamlet is mad. Since he has killed the chancellor, it is for his own safety that we must carry out our plan and send him away to England."

So Hamlet was sent, under the charge of two courtiers who served the king. They bore letters to the English court requiring that Hamlet should be put to death. But Hamlet had the good sense to look at these letters and put in others instead, changing his name to the names of the two courtiers who were so ready to betray him. Then Hamlet escaped on board a pirate ship. The two wicked courtiers left him to his fate, and went on to meet theirs.

Hamlet hurried home, but in the meantime a dreadful thing had happened. Poor, pretty Ophelia, having lost her lover and her father, lost her wits too. She went in sad madness about the court, with weeds and flowers in her hair, singing strange scraps of songs and talking foolish talk with no meaning to it. One day, coming to a  stream where willows grew, she tried to hang a flowery garland on a willow and fell into the water with all her flowers, and so died.

Hamlet had loved her, though his pretended madness had made him hide it. When he came back, he found the king and queen, and the court, weeping at the funeral of his dear love and lady.

Ophelia's brother, Laertes, had also just come to court to ask justice for the death of his father, old Polonius. Now, wild with grief, he leaped into his sister's grave to clasp her in his arms once more.

"I loved her more than forty thousand brothers," cried Hamlet, and leaped into the grave after him. The two fought till they were parted.

Afterward Hamlet begged Laertes to forgive him.

"I could not bear," he said, "that any, even a brother, should seem to love her more than I."

But the wicked Claudius would not let them be friends. He told Laertes how Hamlet had killed old Polonius, and between them they made a plot to slay Hamlet by treachery.

Laertes challenged him to a fencing match. All the court were present. Hamlet had the blunt foil always used in fencing, but Laertes had prepared for himself a sword, sharp and dipped in poison. And the wicked king had a bowl of poisoned wine, which he meant to give poor Hamlet when he grew warm with the swordplay and called for drink.

So Laertes and Hamlet fought, and Laertes, after some fencing, gave Hamlet a sharp sword thrust. Hamlet, angry at this attack—for they had been fencing not to fight, but as play—struggled with Laertes. Both dropped their swords, and when they picked them up again, Hamlet, without noticing it, had exchanged his own blunt sword for Laertes's sharp and poisoned one. With one thrust of it, he pierced Laertes, who fell dead by his own treachery.

At this moment the queen cried out, "The drink, the drink! Oh, my dear Hamlet! I am poisoned!"

She had drunk of the poisoned bowl the king had prepared for Hamlet. The king saw the queen, whom, wicked as he was, he really loved, fall dead by his means.

With the death of his mother and all who had gone before her, Hamlet at last found courage to do the ghost's bidding and avenge his father's murder. (Which, if he had steeled his heart to do long before, all these lives would have been spared and none would have suffered but the wicked king, who well deserved to die.)

Hamlet turned the poisoned sword on the false king.

"Then—venom—do thy work!" he cried, and the king died.

So Hamlet in the end kept the promise he had made his father. And with that accomplished, he himself died. Those who saw him die did so with prayers and tears, for his friends and his people loved him with their whole hearts. Thus ends the tragic tale of Hamlet, prince of Denmark.

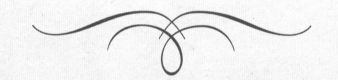

MACBETH

MACBETH

Fair is foul, and foul is fair.

✧

By the pricking of my thumbs,
Something wicked this way comes.

CAST OF CHARACTERS

MACBETH
an army general and chieftain
(lord) of Glamis

LADY MACBETH
wife of Macbeth

DUNCAN
king of Scotland

MALCOLM
older son of Duncan

DONALBAIN
younger son of Duncan

BANQUO
an army general

FLEANCE
Banquo's son

MACDUFF
chieftain of Fife

LADY MACDUFF
wife of Macduff

LENNOX
a Scottish noble

THREE WITCHES

SCENE

SCOTLAND

hen a person is asked to tell the story of Macbeth, he can tell two stories. One is of a man called Macbeth who came to the throne of Scotland in the year of Our Lord 1040 and reigned justly and well for fifteen years or more. This story is part of Scottish history. The other story comes from a place called Imagination; it is gloomy and wonderful, and you shall hear it.

A year or two before Edward the Confessor began to rule England, a battle was won in Scotland against a Norwegian king by two generals named Macbeth and Banquo. After the battle, the generals walked together toward Forres, in Elginshire, where Duncan, king of Scotland, was awaiting them.

While they were crossing a lonely heath, they saw three bearded women, sisters, withered in appearance and wild in their attire.

"Speak, who are you?" demanded Macbeth.

"Hail, Macbeth, chieftain of Glamis," said the first woman.

"Hail, Macbeth, chieftain of Cawdor," said the second woman.

"Hail, Macbeth, king that is to be," said the third woman.

Then Banquo asked, "What of me?" and the third woman replied, "Thou shalt be the father of kings."

"Tell me more," said Macbeth. "By my father's death I am chieftain of Glamis, but the chieftain of Cawdor lives, and the king lives. Speak, I charge you!"

The women replied only by vanishing, as though suddenly mixed with the air.

Banquo and Macbeth knew then that they had been addressed by witches. They were discussing their prophecies when two nobles approached. One of them thanked Macbeth, in the king's name, for his military services, and the other said, "He bade me call you chieftain of Cawdor."

Macbeth then learned that the man who had yesterday held that title was to die for treason, and he could not help thinking, "The third witch called me 'king that is to be.'"

"Banquo," he said, "you see that the witches spoke truth concerning me. Do you not believe that your child and grandchild will be kings?"

Banquo frowned. Duncan had two sons, Malcolm and Donalbain, and he felt it disloyal to hope that his son Fleance should rule Scotland. He told Macbeth that the witches might have intended to tempt them both into villainy by their prophecies. Macbeth, however, thought the prophecy that he should be king too pleasant to keep to himself, and he mentioned it to his wife in a letter.

Lady Macbeth was the granddaughter of a king of Scotland who had died defending his crown against the king who came before Duncan and by whose order her only brother was slain. To her, Duncan was a reminder of bitter wrongs. Her husband had royal blood in his veins, and she was determined that he should be king.

When a messenger came to inform her that Duncan would spend a night in Macbeth's castle, she steeled herself for a cruel act.

When Macbeth arrived, she told him that Duncan must spend a

sunless morrow. She meant that Duncan must die (as that the dead are blind). "We will speak further," said Macbeth uneasily. With his memory full of Duncan's kind words, he would have rather spared his guest.

"Would you live a coward?" demanded Lady Macbeth, who seems to have thought that morality and cowardice were the same.

"I dare do all that may become a man," replied Macbeth; "who dares do more is none."

"Why did you write that letter to me?" she inquired fiercely. With bitter words she egged him on to murder, and with cunning words she showed him how to do it.

After supper Duncan went to bed, and two grooms were placed on guard at his bedroom door.

Lady Macbeth made them drink wine till they were in a stupor. She then took their daggers and would have killed the king herself if his sleeping face had not looked like her father's.

Macbeth came and found the daggers lying by the grooms. Soon with red hands he appeared before his wife, saying, "Methought I heard a voice cry, 'Sleep no more! Macbeth destroys the sleeping.'"

"Wash your hands," said she. "Why did you not leave the daggers by the grooms? Take them back and smear the grooms with blood."

"I dare not," said Macbeth.

His wife dared. She returned to him with hands red as his own, but with a heart less white, she proudly told him, for she scorned his fear.

The murderers heard a knocking, and Macbeth wished it was a knocking that could wake the dead. But it was Macduff, the chieftain of Fife, who had been told by Duncan to visit him early. Macbeth went to him and showed him to the king's room.

Macduff entered and came out again, crying, "O horror! Horror! Horror!"

Macbeth appeared as horror-struck as Macduff, and, pretending that he could not bear to see life in Duncan's murderers, he slew the two grooms with their own daggers before they could proclaim their innocence.

Macbeth's guilt did not shriek out, and he was crowned at Scone. One of Duncan's sons fled to Ireland, the other to England. Macbeth was king. But he was discontented. The prophecy concerning Banquo oppressed his mind. If Fleance were to rule, a son of Macbeth would not rule. Macbeth decided, therefore, to murder both Banquo and his son. He hired two ruffians, who slew Banquo as he was on his way with Fleance to a banquet that Macbeth was giving for his nobles. Fleance escaped.

Meanwhile Macbeth and his queen received their guests very graciously, and he expressed a wish that has been uttered thousands of times since his day: "Now good digestion wait on appetite, and health on both."

"We pray Your Majesty to sit with us," said Lennox, a Scots noble. It was then that the ghost of Banquo entered the banqueting hall and sat in Macbeth's place.

Not noticing the ghost, Macbeth observed that, if Banquo were present, he could say that he had collected under his roof the finest chivalry of Scotland.

The king was again pressed to take a seat. Lennox, who could not see Banquo's ghost, offered Macbeth the chair in which it sat.

But Macbeth, with his eyes of genius, saw the ghost. He saw it like a form of mist and blood, and he demanded passionately, "Which of you have done this?"

Still none saw the ghost but he. To the ghost Macbeth said, "Thou canst not say I did it."

The ghost glided out. Macbeth raised a glass of wine "to the general joy of the whole table, and to our dear friend Banquo, whom we miss."

The toast was drunk as the ghost of Banquo entered for the second time.

"Begone!" cried Macbeth. "You are senseless, mindless! Hide in the earth, thou horrible shadow."

Again none saw the ghost but he.

"What is it Your Majesty sees?" asked one of the nobles.

The queen dared not permit an answer to this question. She hurriedly begged her guests to leave Macbeth, who was a sick man and likely to grow worse if he was obliged to talk.

Macbeth, however, was well enough the next day to converse with the witches whose prophecies had so maddened him.

He found them in a cavern on a thunderous day. They were dancing around a cauldron in which were boiling particles of many strange and horrible creatures, and they knew he was coming before he arrived.

"Answer me what I ask you," said the king.

"Would you rather hear it from us or our masters?" asked the first witch.

"Call them," replied Macbeth.

The witches poured blood into the cauldron and grease into the flame that licked it. A helmeted head appeared with the visor on, so that Macbeth could see only its eyes.

Macbeth began to speak to the head, but the first witch said gravely, "He knows thy thought."

A voice in the helmet said, "Macbeth, beware Macduff, the chieftain of Fife." The head then descended into the cauldron till it disappeared.

"One word more," pleaded Macbeth.

"He will not be commanded," said the first witch. Then a crowned child rose from the cauldron bearing a tree in his hand. The child said:

Macbeth shall be unconquerable till
The Wood of Birnam climbs Dunsinane Hill.

"That will never be," said Macbeth. Then he asked to be told if Banquo's descendants would ever rule Scotland.

The cauldron sank into the earth. Music was heard, and a procession of phantom kings filed past Macbeth. Behind them was Banquo's ghost. In each king Macbeth saw a likeness to Banquo, and he counted eight kings.

Then he was suddenly left alone.

His next act was to send murderers to Macduff's castle. They did not find Macduff, and asked Lady Macduff where he was. She gave a stinging answer, and her questioner called Macduff a traitor. "Thou liest!" shouted Macduff's little son, who was immediately stabbed. With his last breath he told his mother to run. The murderers did not leave the castle with a single person alive.

Macduff was in England with Duncan's son Malcolm when his friend Ross came to tell him that his wife and children were no more. At first Ross dared not speak the truth. But when Malcolm said that England was sending an army into Scotland against Macbeth, Ross blurted out his news, and Macduff cried, "All dead, did you say? All my pretty ones and their mother? Did you say all?"

His sole hope was revenge, but if he could have looked into Macbeth's castle on Dunsinane Hill, he would have seen at work a force more solemn than revenge. Justice was working, for Lady Macbeth was mad. She walked in her sleep, suffering ghastly dreams. She would wash her hands for a quarter of an hour, but after all her washing she would still see a red spot of blood on her skin. It was pitiful to hear her cry that all the perfumes of Arabia could not sweeten her little hand.

"Canst thou not minister to a mind diseased?" inquired Macbeth of the doctor, but the doctor replied that his patient must heal her own mind. This reply made Macbeth scornful of medicine. "Throw physic to the dogs," he said; "I'll none of it."

One day he heard women crying. An officer approached him and said, "The queen, Your Majesty, is dead."

"Out, brief candle," muttered Macbeth, meaning that life was like a candle, at the mercy of a puff of air. He did not weep; he was too familiar with death.

Presently a messenger told him that he saw Birnam Wood on the march. Macbeth called him a liar and a slave, and threatened to hang him if he had made a mistake. "But if you are right you can hang me," said Macbeth.

From the turret windows of Dunsinane castle, Birnam Wood did indeed appear to be marching. Every soldier of the English army held a branch that he had cut from a tree in that wood, and like human trees they climbed Dunsinane Hill.

Macbeth had still his courage. He went to battle to conquer or die, and the first thing he did was to kill the English general's son in single combat. Macbeth then felt that no man could fight him and live. When Macduff came to him blazing for revenge, Macbeth said to him, "Go back; I have spilt too much of your blood already."

"My voice is in my sword," replied Macduff. He hacked at him and bade him yield.

"I will not yield!" said Macbeth, but his last hour had struck. He fell.

Macbeth's men were in retreat when Macduff came to Malcolm, holding Macbeth's head by the hair.

"Hail, king!" he said, and the new king looked at the old.

So Malcolm reigned after Macbeth; but in years that came afterward, the descendants of Banquo were kings.

THE
TEMPEST

THE TEMPEST

Me, poor man—my library
Was dukedom large enough.

CAST OF CHARACTERS

PROSPERO
the exiled duke of Milan
and a sorcerer

MIRANDA
daughter of Prospero

ARIEL
a spirit who serves Prospero

CALIBAN
a monster who serves Prospero

ANTONIO
brother of Prospero and current
duke of Milan

ALONSO
king of Naples

FERDINAND
prince of Naples

SEBASTIAN
brother of King Alonso

GONZALO
a lord who is loyal to
Prospero

SCENE

AN ISLAND IN THE MEDITERRANEAN SEA

rospero, the duke of Milan, was a learned man who lived among his books. He left the running of his dukedom to his brother Antonio, in whom indeed he had complete trust. But that trust was betrayed, for Antonio wanted to wear the duke's crown himself. To gain his ends, he would have killed his brother but for the love the people bore him. However, with the help of Prospero's great enemy Alonso, king of Naples, he managed to get the dukedom with all its honor, power, and riches. For they took Prospero to sea, and when they were far away from land, forced him into a little boat with no tackle, mast, or sail. In their cruelty and hatred, they put his little daughter, Miranda (not yet three years old), into the boat with him. Then they sailed away, leaving them to their fate.

But one of the courtiers was true to his rightful master, Prospero. This worthy lord, whose name was Gonzalo, secretly placed in the boat some fresh water, provisions, and clothes, and what Prospero valued most of all, some of his precious books.

Prospero and his little one landed in safety on an island. Now, this island was enchanted. For years it had lain under the spell of an evil witch, Sycorax, who had imprisoned in the trunks of trees all the good spirits she found there. She died shortly before Prospero was cast on the shore; but the spirits, of whom Ariel was the chief, still remained in their prisons.

Prospero was a great magician, for he had devoted himself to the study of magic during the years he allowed his brother to manage the affairs of Milan. By his art he set free the imprisoned spirits. But he kept them obedient to his will, and they were more truly his loyal subjects than his courtiers in Milan had been, for he treated them kindly as long as they did his bidding, and he exercised his power over them wisely and well. One creature alone he found it necessary to treat with harshness; this was Caliban, the son of the wicked old witch, a hideous, deformed monster, horrible to look on and vicious in all his habits.

When Miranda had grown up into a maiden, sweet and fair to see, it happened that Antonio and Alonso, with Sebastian, his brother, and Ferdinand, his son, were at sea together with old Gonzalo. Their ship came near Prospero's island. Prospero, knowing they were close, raised so great a storm that the sailors on board gave themselves up for lost.

Prince Ferdinand leaped into the sea and was drowned—or so his grieving father thought. But Ariel brought him safe ashore. All the rest of the crew, although they were washed overboard, landed unhurt in different parts of the island. The good ship herself, which they all thought had been wrecked, lay at anchor in the harbor where Ariel had brought her. Such wonders could Prospero and his spirits perform.

While the tempest was raging, Prospero showed his daughter the brave ship laboring in the rough seas and told her that it was filled with living human beings like themselves. She, feeling sorry for them, begged him who had raised this storm to calm it. Her father bade her to have no fear, for he intended to save every one of them.

Then, for the first time, he told her the story of his life and hers. He explained that he had caused this storm to rise in order that his enemies, Antonio and Alonso, might be delivered into his hands.

When he had made an end of his story, he charmed her into sleep, for Ariel was at hand and he had work for him to do. Ariel, who longed for his freedom, grumbled to be kept in drudgery. Angry, Prospero reminded him of all the sufferings he had undergone when Sycorax ruled in the land and of the debt of gratitude he owed to the master who had made those sufferings end. Ariel ceased to complain and promised faithfully to do whatever Prospero might command.

"Do so," said Prospero, "and in two days I will discharge thee."

Then he bade Ariel take the form of a water nymph and sent him in search of the young prince. Ariel, invisible to Ferdinand, hovered near him, singing the while:

Come unto these yellow sands,
And then take hands,
Courtsied when you have and kiss'd—
The wild waves whist—
Foot it featly here and there,
And, sweet sprites, the burden bear.

Ferdinand followed the magical singing. Then the song changed to a solemn tune, and the words brought grief to his heart and tears to his eyes, for thus they ran:

Full fathom five thy father lies.
Of his bones are coral made;
Those are pearls that were his eyes;
Nothing of him that doth fade

But doth suffer a sea-change

Into something rich and strange.

Sea-nymphs hourly ring his knell.

Hark, now I hear them. Ding-dong, bell.

Ariel led the spellbound prince into the presence of Prospero and Miranda. Then, behold! All happened as Prospero desired. For Miranda, who had never, since she could first remember, seen any human being save her father, looked on the youthful prince with reverence in her eyes and love in her secret heart.

"I might call him," she said, "a thing divine, for nothing natural I ever saw so noble!"

And Ferdinand, beholding her beauty with wonder and delight, exclaimed, "Most sure the goddess on whom these airs attend!"

Scarcely had they exchanged half a dozen sentences before he vowed to make her his queen if she were willing. Prospero, though secretly delighted, pretended to be angry.

"You come here as a spy," he said to Ferdinand. "I will chain your neck and feet together, and you shall feed on fresh-water mussels, withered roots and husk, and have seawater to drink. Follow."

"No," said Ferdinand, and drew his sword. But at that instant Prospero charmed him so that he stood there like a statue, still as stone. In terror Miranda begged her father to have mercy on her lover. But he harshly refused her and made Ferdinand follow him to his dwelling. There he set the prince to work, making him move thousands of heavy logs of timber and pile them up. Ferdinand patiently obeyed, and thought his toil well repaid by the sympathy of the sweet Miranda.

She would have helped him in his hard work, but he would not let her. He could not keep from her the secret of his love. She, hearing it, rejoiced and promised to be his wife.

Then Prospero released him from his servitude, and glad at heart, he gave his consent to their marriage.

"Take her," he said, "she is thine own."

Meanwhile, in another part of the island, Antonio and Sebastian were plotting the murder of Alonso, the king of Naples. They thought Ferdinand was dead, so Sebastian would succeed to the throne on Alonso's death. They would have carried out their wicked plan while their victim was asleep except Ariel woke Alonso just in time.

Many tricks did Ariel play on them. Once he set a banquet before them, and just as they were about to gorge themselves, he appeared to them amid thunder and lightning, and immediately the banquet disappeared. Then Ariel scolded them for their sins and vanished too.

Prospero by his enchantments drew everyone to the grove outside his rooms, where they waited, trembling and afraid. At last they bitterly repented all their sins.

Prospero decided to make one last use of his magic power. "And then," said he, "I'll break my staff and deeper than did ever plummet sound I'll drown my book."

So he made heavenly music to fill the air and appeared to them in his proper shape as the duke of Milan. Because they repented, he forgave them and told them the story of his life since they had cruelly abandoned him and his baby daughter to the mercy of wind and waves. Alonso, who seemed sorriest of them all, lamented the loss of his heir. But Prospero drew back a curtain and showed him Ferdinand and Miranda playing chess. Great was Alonso's joy to greet his beloved son again. And when he heard that the fair maid with whom Ferdinand was playing was Prospero's daughter and that the young folks had pledged to marry, he said,

"Give me your hands. Let grief and sorrow still embrace his heart that doth not wish you joy."

So all ended happily. The ship was safe in the harbor, and the next day they all set sail for Naples, where Ferdinand and Miranda were to be married. Ariel gave them calm seas and favorable winds, and many were the rejoicings at the wedding.

Prospero went back to his own dukedom, where he was welcomed with great joy by his faithful subjects. He practiced the arts of magic no more, but his life was happy. Not only had he regained his dukedom, but when his bitterest foes, who had done him deadly wrong, lay at his mercy, he took no vengeance on them, but nobly forgave them.

As for Ariel, Prospero made him free as air so that he could wander where he would and sing with a light heart his sweet song:

Where the bee sucks, there suck I:
In a cowslip's bell I lie;
There I couch when owls do cry.
On the bat's back I do fly
After summer merrily.
Merrily, merrily shall I live now
Under the blossom that hangs on the bough.

MUCH ADO
ABOUT NOTHING

MUCH ADO ABOUT NOTHING

I had rather hear my dog bark at a crow than a man swear he loves me.

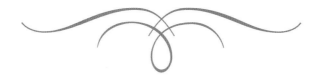

CAST OF CHARACTERS

LEONATO
governor of Messina

HERO
daughter of Leonato

BEATRICE
niece of Leonato

DON PEDRO
prince of Aragon

CLAUDIO
officer in Don Pedro's army

BENEDICK
officer in Don Pedro's army

DON JOHN
Don Pedro's half brother

BORACHIO
a citizen of Messina

CONRADE
friend of Borachio

MARGARET
maid of Hero

URSULA
companion of Hero

DOGBERRY
a constable

FRIAR FRANCIS
a priest

SCENE

ITALY

n Sicily is a town called Messina. It's the scene of a curious storm in a teacup that raged several hundred years ago.

It began with sunshine. Don Pedro, prince of Aragon, had gained complete victory over his foes. Feeling happy after the fatigues of war, Don Pedro came for a holiday to Messina. In his company were his stepbrother, Don John, and two young Italian lords, Benedick and Claudio.

Benedick was a merry chatterbox who was determined never to marry. Claudio, on the other hand, no sooner arrived in Messina than he fell in love with Hero, the daughter of Leonato, governor of Messina.

One July day, a perfumer called Borachio was burning dried lavender in a musty room in Leonato's house when the sound of conversation floated through the open window.

"Give me your candid opinion of Hero," Claudio asked.

"Too short and brown for praise" was Benedick's reply, "but alter her color or height, and you spoil her."

"In my eyes she is the sweetest of women," said Claudio.

"Not in mine," retorted Benedick, "and I have no need for glasses. She is like the last day of December compared with the first of May if you set her beside her cousin. Unfortunately, the Lady Beatrice is a fury."

Beatrice was Leonato's niece. She amused herself by saying sharp and witty things about Benedick, who called her Dear Lady Disdain. She liked to say that she was born under a dancing star and so could never be dull.

Claudio and Benedick were still talking when Don Pedro came up and said good-humoredly, "Well, gentlemen, what's the secret?"

"I am longing," answered Benedick, "for Your Grace to command me to tell."

"I charge you then, on your allegiance, to tell me," said Don Pedro, playing along with the joke.

"I can be as dumb as a mute," apologized Benedick to Claudio, "but His Grace commands my speech." To Don Pedro he said, "Claudio is in love with Hero, Leonato's short daughter."

Don Pedro was pleased, for he admired Hero and was fond of Claudio. When Benedick had left, he said to Claudio, "Be steadfast in your love for Hero, and I will help you to win her. Tonight her father gives a masquerade ball. I will pretend I am Claudio and tell her how I love her. If she be pleased, I will go to her father and ask his consent to your union."

Most men like to do their own wooing, but if you fall in love with a governor's only daughter, you are fortunate to have a prince plead for you.

Claudio then was fortunate. But he was unfortunate as well, for he had an enemy who pretended to be a friend. This enemy was Don Pedro's stepbrother, Don John, who was jealous of Claudio because Don Pedro preferred him to Don John.

It was to Don John that Borachio came with the interesting conversation that he had overheard.

"I shall have some fun at that masquerade myself," said Don John when Borachio finished his story.

On the night of the masquerade, Don Pedro, masked and pretending he was Claudio, asked Hero if he might walk with her.

When they had left, Don John went up to Claudio and said, "Signor Benedick, I believe?"

"The same," fibbed Claudio.

"I should be much obliged then," said Don John, "if you would use your influence with my brother to cure him of his love for Hero. She is beneath him in rank."

"How do you know he loves her?" inquired Claudio.

"I heard him swear his affection" was the reply, and Borachio chimed in with "So did I too."

Claudio was then left to himself, and his thought was that his prince had betrayed him. "Farewell, Hero," he muttered; "I was a fool to trust a messenger."

Meanwhile Beatrice and Benedick (who was masked) were having a brisk exchange of opinions.

"Did Benedick ever make you laugh?" asked she.

"Who is Benedick?" he inquired.

"A prince's jester," replied Beatrice.

She spoke to Benedick so sharply that he later declared, "I would not marry her if she stood to inherit the Garden of Eden."

Meanwhile Don Pedro had carried out his plan to the letter. He brought the light back to Claudio's eyes in a twinkling when he appeared with Leonato and Hero, and asked, "Claudio, when would you like to go to church?"

"Tomorrow" was the prompt answer. "Time goes on crutches till I marry Hero."

"Give her a week, my dear son," said Leonato, and Claudio's heart thumped with joy.

"And now," said the amiable Don Pedro, "we must find a wife for Signor Benedick. It is a task for Hercules."

"I will help you," said Leonato, "if I have to sit up ten nights."

Then Hero spoke. "I will do what I can, my lord, to find a good husband for Beatrice."

Thus, with happy laughter, ended the masquerade.

Borachio cheered up Don John by laying another plan before him. He would persuade both Claudio and Don Pedro that Hero was a fickle girl who was toying with them both. Don John agreed to this plan of hate.

Don Pedro, on the other hand, had devised a cunning plan of love. "If," he said to Leonato, "we pretend, when Beatrice is near enough to overhear us, that Benedick is pining for her love, she will pity him, see his good qualities, and love him. And if, when Benedick thinks we don't know he is listening, we say how sad it is that the beautiful Beatrice should be in love with a heartless scoffer like Benedick, he will certainly be on his knees before her in a week or less."

So one day when Benedick was reading in a summer house, Claudio sat outside with Leonato and said loudly, "Your daughter told me about a letter Beatrice wrote."

"Letter!" exclaimed Leonato. "She will get up twenty times in the night and write goodness knows what. But once Hero peeped and saw the words 'Benedick and Beatrice' on the sheet, and then Beatrice tore it up."

"Hero told me," said Claudio, "that she cried, 'O sweet Benedick!'"

Benedick was touched by this incredible story, which he was vain enough to believe. "She is fair and good," he said to himself. "I must not seem proud. I feel that I love her. People will laugh, of course; but their paper bullets will do me no harm."

At this moment Beatrice came to the summer house and said, "Against my will, I have come to tell you that dinner is ready."

"Fair Beatrice, I thank you," said Benedick.

"I took no more pains to come than you take pains to thank me" was the reply, intended to freeze him.

But it did not freeze him. It warmed him. The meaning he squeezed out of her rude speech was that she was delighted to come to him.

Hero had the task of melting the heart of Beatrice. One day she said to her maid Margaret, "Run into the parlor and whisper to Beatrice that Ursula and I are talking about her in the orchard."

She felt sure that Beatrice would listen in on their conversation. In that way she would overhear what was meant for her ears as well as if she had made an appointment to talk with her cousin.

In the orchard was a bower, screened from the sun by honeysuckles. Beatrice entered it a few minutes after Margaret told her Hero and Ursula were talking about her.

"But are you sure," asked Ursula, who was one of Hero's companions,

"that Benedick loves Beatrice so devotedly?"

"So say the prince and my betrothed," replied Hero, "and they wished me to tell her, but I said 'No! Let Benedick get over it.'"

"Why did you say that?"

"Because Beatrice is unbearably proud. Her eyes sparkle with disdain and scorn. She is too conceited to love. I should not like to see her making game of poor Benedick's love."

"I don't agree with you," said Ursula. "I think your cousin is too clear-sighted not to see the merits of Benedick."

"He is the finest man in Italy, except for Claudio," said Hero.

The talkers then left the orchard. Beatrice, excited and tender, stepped out of the summer house, saying to herself, "Poor dear Benedick, be true to me, and your love shall tame this wild heart of mine."

We now return to the plan of hate.

The night before Claudio's wedding, Don John entered a room in which Don Pedro and Claudio were talking, and asked Claudio if he intended to be married tomorrow.

"You know he does!" said Don Pedro.

"He may know differently," said Don John, "when he has seen what I will show him if he will follow me."

They followed him into the garden, where they saw a lady leaning out of Hero's window talking love to Borachio.

Claudio thought the lady was Hero and said, "I will shame her for it tomorrow!"

Don Pedro thought she was Hero too. But it was not Hero; it was Margaret.

Don John chuckled when Claudio and Don Pedro left the garden. Then he gave Borachio a purse containing a thousand ducats.

The money made Borachio feel quite jolly and reckless. Walking in the street with his friend Conrade, he boasted of his wealth and told him what he had done to earn it.

A watchman overheard them. He thought that a man who had been paid a thousand ducats for villainy should be punished. He therefore arrested Borachio and Conrade, who spent the rest of the night in prison.

Before noon of the next day, half the aristocrats in Messina were at church. Hero was there in her wedding dress, no cloud on her pretty face or in her frank and shining eyes.

The priest was Friar Francis.

Turning to Claudio, he said, "You come hither, my lord, to marry this lady?"

"No!" contradicted Claudio.

Leonato thought Claudio was quibbling over grammar. He told the friar, "You should have asked 'Do you come to *be* married?'"

Friar Francis turned to Hero. "Lady," he said, "you come hither to be married to this count?"

"I do," replied Hero.

"If either of you know any impediment to this marriage, I charge you to utter it," said the friar.

"Do you know of any, Hero?" asked Claudio.

"None," said she.

"Know you of any, Count?" demanded the friar.

"I dare reply for him, none," said Leonato.

Claudio exclaimed bitterly, "O! What will not men dare say! Sir," he asked Leonato, "will you give me your daughter?"

"As freely," replied Leonato, "as God gave her to me."

"And what can I give you," asked Claudio, "which is worthy of this gift?"

"Nothing," said Don Pedro, "unless you give the gift back to the giver."

"Sweet prince, you teach me," said Claudio. "There, Leonato, take her back."

These brutal words were followed by others that flew from Claudio, Don Pedro, and Don John.

Hero defended herself as long as she could, then she swooned. All her persecutors left the church except her father, who was fooled by the accusations against her and cried, "Hence from her! Let her die!"

But with his clear eyes that probed the soul, Friar Francis saw that Hero was blameless. "She is innocent," he said. "A thousand signs have told me so."

Hero revived under his kind gaze. Her father, confused and angry, knew not what to think. The friar said, "They have left her as one dead with shame. Let us pretend that she is dead until the truth is declared and slander turns to remorse."

"The friar advises well," said Benedick. Then Hero was led away, and

Beatrice and Benedick remained alone in the church.

Benedick saw that Beatrice had been weeping bitterly and long.

"Surely I do believe your fair cousin is wronged," he said. She still wept.

"Is it not strange," asked Benedick gently, "that I love nothing in the world as well as you?"

"It were as possible for me to say I loved nothing as well as you," said Beatrice, "but I do not say it. I am sorry for my cousin."

"Tell me what I can do for you," said Benedick.

"Kill Claudio."

"Ha! Not for the wide world," said Benedick.

"Your refusal kills me," said Beatrice. "Farewell."

"Enough! I will challenge him," cried Benedick.

Meanwhile Borachio and Conrade were in prison, where they were questioned by a constable called Dogberry. The watchman gave evidence that Borachio had said that he had received a thousand ducats for conspiring against Hero.

Leonato did not know any of this, but he was now thoroughly convinced of Hero's innocence. He played the part of bereaved father very well, and when Don Pedro and Claudio called on him, he said, "You have slandered my child to death, and I challenge you to combat."

"I cannot fight an old man," said Claudio.

"You could kill a girl," sneered Leonato, and Claudio blushed.

Hot words grew from hot words. Both Don Pedro and Claudio were feeling scorched when Leonato left the room and Benedick entered.

"The old man," said Claudio, "was like to have snapped my nose off."

"You are a villain!" said Benedick shortly. "Fight me when and with what weapon you please, or I call you a coward."

Claudio was astounded but said, "I'll meet you. Nobody shall say I can't carve a calf's head."

It was time for Don Pedro to receive officials and hear complaints. The prince sat down in a chair of state and prepared his mind for justice.

The door soon opened to admit Dogberry and his prisoners.

"What offense," said Don Pedro, "are these men charged with?"

Borachio thought it time to make a clean breast of it. He laid the blame on Don John, who had disappeared.

"The lady Hero being dead," he said, "I desire nothing but the reward of a murderer."

Claudio heard this news with anguish and deep repentance.

He said to Leonato, "Borachio makes clear your daughter's innocence. Choose your revenge."

"Leonato," said Don Pedro humbly, "I am ready for any penance you may impose."

"I ask you both," said Leonato, "to proclaim my daughter's innocence and to honor her tomb by singing her praise before it. As for you, Claudio, I have this to say: my brother has a daughter so like Hero that she might be a copy of her. Marry her, and my vengeful feelings die."

"Noble sir," said Claudio, "I am yours."

Claudio then went to his room and composed a solemn song. Going to the church with Don Pedro and his attendants, he sang it before the monument of Leonato's family. When he had ended, he said, "Good night, Hero. Yearly will I do this."

Gravely, as his heart was Hero's, Claudio prepared to marry a girl he did not love. He was told to meet her in Leonato's house, where he was shown into a room. Then Antonio (Leonato's brother) and several masked ladies entered. Friar Francis, Leonato, and Benedick were also present.

Antonio led one of the ladies toward Claudio.

"Sweet," said the young man, "let me see your face."

"Swear first to marry her," said Leonato.

"Give me your hand," said Claudio to the lady. "Before this holy friar I swear to marry you if you will be my wife."

"Alive I was your wife," said the lady as she drew off her mask.

"Another Hero!" exclaimed Claudio.

"Hero died," explained Leonato, "only while slander lived."

The friar was about to marry the reconciled pair, but Benedick interrupted him. "Softly, Friar; which of these ladies is Beatrice?"

At this Beatrice unmasked, and Benedick said, "You love me, don't you?"

"Only moderately" was the reply. "Do you love me?"

"Moderately," answered Benedick.

"I was told you were well-nigh dead for me," remarked Beatrice.

"Of you I was told the same," said Benedick.

"Here's a paper in your own hand to prove your love," said Claudio, producing a feeble sonnet that Benedick had written to his sweetheart.

"And here," said Hero, "is a tribute to Benedick that I picked out of the pocket of Beatrice."

"A miracle!" exclaimed Benedick. "Our hands are against our hearts! Come, I will marry you, Beatrice."

"You shall be my husband to save your life" was her answer.

Benedick kissed her on the mouth, and the friar married them after he had married Claudio and Hero.

"How is Benedick, the married man?" asked Don Pedro.

"Too happy to be made unhappy," replied Benedick. "Crack what jokes you will. As for you, Claudio, I had hoped to run you through the body, but as you are now my kinsman, live whole and love my cousin. Come, come, let's dance!"

And dance they did. Not even the news of the capture of Don John was able to stop the flying feet of the happy lovers, for revenge is not sweet against an evil man who has failed to do harm.

BIOGRAPHY OF WILLIAM SHAKESPEARE

nown to many as simply the Bard, William Shakespeare was one of the greatest writers in the English language and certainly the greatest playwright the world has ever known. Yet we know amazingly little about him. We don't even know exactly when he was born.

What we do know is that William Shakespeare was baptized on April 26, 1564, in the town of Stratford-upon-Avon in England. That year, nearly two-thirds of English infants died, so it would have been important to get the baby baptized quickly—say, three days after he was born. So scholars have chosen April 23 as Shakespeare's birthday. He would die on the exact same day fifty-two years later.

Shakespeare's mother, Mary Arden, came from an old and prominent family. His father, John Shakespeare, was a glove maker. Many people wore gloves in the sixteenth century, and he was very successful. He became an important man in Stratford, serving on the town council. He rose to the position of high bailiff, which was something like the mayor. One of his jobs as high bailiff was to welcome (and pay) the acting companies that came to Stratford. Many people think this might have been Shakespeare's first exposure to theater.

When it was time for an education, young William probably attended Stratford grammar school, which still stands today as the King Edward VI School. He went to school from six in the morning to five or six at night. What did young William study for twelve hours a day? Latin. A lot of Latin. That might not sound very useful. But he would have been expected to recite in Latin—good vocal training for a future actor—and teachers often let students act in classical plays.

Shakespeare probably left school when he was fourteen. At age eighteen he married Anne Hathaway, who was twenty-six. (Their marriage bond is issued to "William Shagspere" and "Anne Hathwey." Elizabethans weren't as fussy about spelling as we are today. In fact, of the six surviving signatures of William Shakespeare's, no two are exactly alike.) Anne and William had three children: Susanna in 1583 and twins, Judith and Hamnet, in 1585.

There are two periods in Shakespeare's life that historians call "the lost years," stretches of time when we know almost nothing about him. The first is 1578 to 1582. The second is 1585 to 1592. At some point during this time, Shakespeare left his family in Stratford to become a playwright and actor in London. How? Shakespeare biographer Bill Bryson shares one intriguing theory. In 1587, when Shakespeare was twenty-three, one of the prominent acting troupes of the day, the Queen's Men, was touring the countryside. One of their leading men, William Knell, got into a fight with a fellow actor. Knell was stabbed through the neck and killed—which left the Queen's Men one man short.

Was the company looking for new talent when they came through Stratford? Did Shakespeare, fondly remembering the plays he saw as a child, race to join up? We have no idea. But by 1592, Shakespeare was definitely in London and writing plays. Unfortunately, in 1593, just as things were going well for Shakespeare, London theaters closed due to an outbreak of bubonic plague. The plague would eventually kill about 5 percent of the city's population. But Shakespeare made good use of the time off by turning to poetry. Shakespeare wrote *Venus and Adonis*, his first long, published poem. It was dedicated to a nobleman, Henry Wriothesley, Earl of Southampton.

The earl became Shakespeare's patron, which meant he gave Shakespeare money to write. Shakespeare began to compose sonnets, fourteen-line poems that follow a precise rhyming scheme and structure. In his lifetime Shakespeare would write 154 sonnets.

In 1594 the theaters reopened. Shakespeare was now part of a theater company called the Lord Chamberlain's Men. They were given that name in honor of their patron, Henry Carey, 1st Baron Hunsdon, the then Lord Chamberlain, who was in charge of entertainment at Elizabeth I's court. The company included Richard Burbage, who was the first actor to play many of Shakespeare's most famous parts. We know that Shakespeare also performed in his plays, as he is one of three actors listed as being paid for a Christmas performance at court.

Shakespeare's only son, Hamnet, died in 1596 at the age of eleven. We don't know how he died or how his father felt about it. But we do know that even though he didn't live with them, Shakespeare was still connected to his family in Stratford, because the following year he bought a big house there called the New Place. The Lord Chamberlain's Men also had new lodgings. They had been performing at the Theatre in London.

They owned the building but not the land on which it stood. That year the landlord raised their rent, and they had to move. But they didn't leave the Theatre behind; they took it with them—every board and nail. Over several weeks they moved pieces of the old theater across the river, where they rebuilt it as the Globe. At that time the Globe was the finest theater yet built. It was an open-air theater hexagonal in shape, and the stage was in the center. It had three stories and could hold more than fifteen hundred people.

Two more deaths affected Shakespeare around this time. First, his father died in 1601, the same year he is thought to have written *Hamlet*, which begins with the death of a father. Two years later Queen Elizabeth I died. As she had no children, the throne was left to James of Scotland. King James I was very fond of theater, and Shakespeare's company thrived, changing their name to the King's Men. They rented London's first permanently enclosed theater, Blackfriars. This theater had a roof to keep out the weather, so the company could perform all year round.

Over the next several years Shakespeare would write some of the most powerful dramas ever staged: *Othello, King Lear, Macbeth*. The plague returned to London, closing its theaters until 1610. This may be what caused Shakespeare to leave London and finally return home to his family in Stratford. He would write one last masterpiece, *The Tempest*, about a duke who is also a magician living on an enchanted island. At the end of the play, he, too, returns home. But he gives up his powers to do so, breaking his magic staff and drowning his book of spells. It's hard not to wonder if that is how Shakespeare felt when he left the magical world of the theater.

Shakespeare died on April 23, 1616, at the age of fifty-two. In his will he left a good sum of money, four houses, and land. Strangely, he left his wife, Anne, the "second-best bed." Why not the best bed? Why no kind words written to his wife in the will, which was typical for the times? Perhaps Shakespeare did not have a happy marriage, or perhaps he was just too ill to write any more poetry. He was buried at Holy Trinity Church in Stratford. At his grave, there is a sign that reads:

> Good friend, for Jesus' sake forebeare
> To digg the dust enclosed heare;
> Bleste be the man that spares thes stones,
> And curst be he that moves my bones

Thousands of plays were written during the Elizabethan era, but very few have survived. Shakespeare's plays might have been lost to us too. But in 1623, John Heminges and Henry Condell, two actors in the original Lord Chamberlain's Men, brought thirty-six of Shakespeare's plays together in what is known as the First Folio. They printed eight hundred copies, selling them for one pound each. In 2006 a complete copy of the First Folio was sold for two and a half million pounds—or around four million dollars.

But the true value of Shakespeare's plays is in the joy they have given readers and audiences for centuries. Their worth lies in the brilliant language, in the deep knowledge of how human beings feel and think, and in an astonishing collection of characters: heroic kings and treacherous villains, lovers and clowns, fairies and philosophers—all created in the mind of one man, William Shakespeare.

TIMELINE

here is no record of the first performances of any of Shakespeare's plays. Scholars use references within the plays, diaries, and letters to determine roughly the order in which they were written.

⤷ **1558** ⟿

✦ Elizabeth I becomes queen of England.

⤷ **1564** ⟿

✦ William Shakespeare is born in Stratford-upon-Avon in England.

⤷ **1571** ⟿

✦ Shakespeare (probably) starts school around age seven.

⤷ **1578–1582** ⟿

✦ The first "lost years." No one knows much about Shakespeare's life during this time.

⤷ **1582** ⟿

✦ Shakespeare marries Anne Hathaway.

⤷ **1583** ⟿

✦ Shakespeare's first child, Susanna, is born.

∽ 1585 ∾

✦ Anne Hathaway gives birth to twins: son, Hamnet, and daughter, Judith.

✦ Sir Walter Raleigh sends a new expedition to Virginia, then an English settlement in America.

✦ Queen Elizabeth breaks with Spain and allies with Dutch Protestant forces. In response, Spain's Philip II seizes all English ships in Spanish ports.

∽ 1585–1592 ∾

✦ The second period of "lost years." At some point Shakespeare leaves Stratford to work as a playwright and actor in London.

∽ 1586 ∾

✦ Mary Queen of Scots is found guilty of conspiring to assassinate her cousin, Elizabeth I.

∽ 1587 ∾

✦ Mary Queen of Scots is executed.

✦ Philip II of Spain prepares a fleet to invade England.

∽ 1588 ∾

✦ The "invincible" Spanish Armada, a fleet of 130 ships, sails to attack England. A great storm sinks many of the ships, which helps the English defeat the Spanish forces.

+ Christopher Marlowe's *The Tragical History of Dr. Faustus* is performed by the Admiral's Men. Born the same year as Shakespeare, Marlowe was one of the most successful playwrights of his day.

⌘ 1590 ⌘

+ The bubonic plague, known as the Black Death, reaches Rome.

⌘ 1592 ⌘

+ Shakespeare's popular trilogy *Henry VI, Part I, Part II*, and *Part III* is thought to be performed.

⌘ 1593 ⌘

+ London theaters are closed due to an outbreak of bubonic plague.
+ *Venus and Adonis*, Shakespeare's first long, published poem, is printed.
+ Shakespeare begins what will become a collection of 154 sonnets.
+ Playwright Christopher Marlowe is killed in a tavern brawl at the age of twenty-nine.

⌘ 1594 ⌘

+ London theaters reopen.
+ The Lord Chamberlain's Men, a theater troupe, is founded. Its members include actor Richard Burbage and William Shakespeare.

∽ 1595 ∽

✦ Spain attacks England's coast, burning the town of Penzance.

✦ Around this time, Shakespeare is thought to have written *Love's Labour's Lost, King John, Richard II, A Midsummer Night's Dream,* and *Romeo and Juliet.*

∽ 1596 ∽

✦ Shakespeare's only son, Hamnet, dies at the age of eleven.

∽ 1597 ∽

✦ Shakespeare buys the New Place in Stratford. Around this time, he is thought to have written *The Merchant of Venice* and *Henry IV, Part I.*

✦ Spain's King Philip II sends a second armada to attack England. Once again a storm scatters the ships.

∽ 1598 ∽

✦ Shakespeare is listed as an actor in Ben Jonson's *Every Man in His Humor.*

✦ King Philip II dies.

✺ 1599 ✺

✦ The Lord Chamberlain's Men build the Globe, a wooden theater in London. *Julius Caesar* is performed there on September 21.

✺ 1600–1601 ✺

✦ Shakespeare's father dies.
✦ Shakespeare writes *Hamlet.*
✦ The earl of Essex rebels against Elizabeth I and is executed for treason. Shakespeare's patron, the Earl of Southampton, takes part in the rebellion but is spared.

✺ 1603 ✺

✦ Elizabeth I dies. King James ascends the throne. The Lord Chamberlain's Men change their name to the King's Men.

✺ 1605 ✺

✦ Shakespeare writes *King Lear,* as well as *Macbeth,* a play set in Scotland in honor of the king's ancestry.

✺ 1608 ✺

✦ The King's Men begin performing at Blackfriars, an indoor theater in London.
✦ The plague returns, closing all of London's theaters until early 1610.

1609

✦ Publisher Thomas Thorpe prints a collection of Shakespeare's sonnets.

1610

✦ Around this time, Shakespeare leaves London and moves back to Stratford.

1612–1613

✦ Shakespeare writes his final plays, including *Henry VIII* and the now-lost *Cardenio*.

1613

✦ The Globe catches fire and burns to the ground.

1614

✦ The Globe reopens.

1616

✦ William Shakespeare dies.

1623

✦ John Heminges and Henry Condell, Shakespeare's former colleagues in the King's Men, collect thirty-six of Shakespeare's plays and publish them as the First Folio.

RECOMMENDED READING

BOOKS ABOUT THE PLAYS

The Riverside Shakespeare, 2nd edition, edited by G. Blakemore Evans (Houghton Mifflin, 1996).

An annotated collection of the complete works, including two recently attributed to Shakespeare: *Edward III* and *Sir Thomas More*. Difficult words are explained at the bottom of each page.

Shakespeare's Words: A Glossary and Language Companion, by David Crystal and Ben Crystal (Penguin, 2002).

A glossary of nearly fourteen thousand words and meanings that are frequently misunderstood by the modern reader.

BOOKS ABOUT THE LIFE OF SHAKESPEARE

Who Was William Shakespeare?, by Celeste Davidson Mannis, illustrated by John O'Brien (Grosset & Dunlap, 2006).

Part of the popular Who Was? series, this lively biography tells young readers the story of Shakespeare's life and times.

Shakespeare: DK Eyewitness Books (DK Eyewitness Books, 2015).

A richly illustrated survey of the life and times of Shakespeare.

William Shakespeare & the Globe, by Aliki (HarperCollins, 2000).

A charmingly illustrated life of Shakespeare that includes a chronology, fun Shakespeare sites to visit, and the story of how the present-day Globe was built.

Bard of Avon: The Story of William Shakespeare, by Diane Stanley and Peter Vennema, illustrated by Diane Stanley (HarperCollins, 1998).

A lovely picture book on the life of Shakespeare, suitable for younger readers.

MAKING SHAKESPEARE FUN FOR KIDS

BOOKS

Brick Shakespeare: Four Tragedies & Four Comedies, by John McCann, Monica Sweeney, and Becky Thomas (Skyhorse; Box Har/Ps edition, 2014).

Four tragedies and four comedies depicted scene by scene by Lego minifigures. Lines from the plays form the text.

How to Teach Your Children Shakespeare, by Ken Ludwig (Broadway, 2014).

This book explores twenty-five of Shakespeare's great speeches. Ludwig

demystifies the language, letting kids progress from reciting classic lines to complete speeches from *Hamlet*.

No Fear Shakespeare Graphic Novels (SparkNotes, 2008).
Starkly vivid graphic novels based on the plays, created by SparkNotes.

The BBC Television Shakespeare

In the 1970s and '80s, the BBC produced every Shakespeare play. Some of the productions don't age well, but others are excellent. A good resource if you need a play that is rarely performed.

The Reduced Shakespeare Company—The Complete Works of William Shakespeare (abridged)

Three actors, thirty-six plays, ninety minutes. High speed and very funny.

Shakespeare: The Animated Tales

Twelve Shakespeare classics in condensed form, recommended for children eight to twelve.

Absolute Shakespeare, www.absoluteshakespeare.com
This fabulous site has everything from summaries to scholarly essays about the plays. It also includes famous quotes, a useful glossary, and fun images.

The Folger Shakespeare Library, www.folger.edu
Home to the largest and finest collection of Shakespeare materials in the world. The website includes specific resources for both teachers and students.

The Royal Shakespeare Company, www.rsc.org.uk
The website for the most famous Shakespeare company in the world includes a wealth of educational material about Shakespeare's plays and life.

Shakespeare Online, www.shakespeare-online.com
Named by Microsoft as one of the top ten internet sites for students, Shakespeare Online is packed with information on everything from how to pronounce "Jacques" to discussions of disease imagery in *Hamlet*.